INTRODU

Mr
Hoppy

Alfie

Mrs
Silver

Pet-shop
Owner

The
Tortoise-catcher

ROALD DAHL

ESIO TROT

ILLUSTRATED BY QUENTIN BLAKE

PUFFIN

Find out more about Roald Dahl
by visiting the website at
roalddahl.com

PUFFIN BOOKS

Published by the Penguin Group
Penguin Books Ltd, 80 Strand, London WC2R ORL, England
Penguin Group (USA) Inc., 375 Hudson Street, New York, New York 10014, USA
Penguin Group (Canada), 90 Eglinton Avenue East, Suite 700, Toronto, Ontario, Canada M4P 2Y3
(a division of Pearson Penguin Canada Inc.)
Penguin Ireland, 25 St Stephen's Green, Dublin 2, Ireland (a division of Penguin Books Ltd)
Penguin Group (Australia), 707 Collins Street, Melbourne, Victoria 3008, Australia (a division of Pearson Australia Group Pty Ltd)
Penguin Books India Pvt Ltd, 11 Community Centre, Panchsheel Park, New Delhi – 110 017, India
Penguin Group (NZ), 67 Apollo Drive, Rosedale, Auckland 0632, New Zealand (a division of Pearson New Zealand Ltd)
Penguin Books (South Africa) (Pty) Ltd, Block D, Rosebank Office Park, 181 Jan Smuts Avenue,
Parktown North, Gauteng 2193, South Africa

Penguin Books Ltd, Registered Offices: 80 Strand, London WC2R ORL, England

puffinbooks.com

First published by Jonathan Cape Ltd 1990

Published in Puffin Books 1991
This edition published 2013
007

Text copyright © Roald Dahl Nominee Ltd, 1990
Illustrations copyright © Quentin Blake, 1990
The moral right of the author and illustrator has been asserted
All rights reserved

Set in Monotype Baskerville
Printed in Great Britain by Clays Ltd, St Ives plc

British Library Cataloguing in Publication Data
A CIP catalogue record for this book is available from the British Library

ISBN: 978-0-141-34649-6

www.greenpenguin.co.uk

MIX
Paper from
responsible sources
FSC
www.fsc.org   FSC™ C018179

Penguin Books is committed to a sustainable
future for our business, our readers and our planet.
This book is made from Forest Stewardship
Council™ certified paper.

To Clover and Luke

Author's Note

Some years ago, when my own children were small, we usually kept a tortoise or two in the garden. In those days, a pet tortoise was a common sight crawling about on the family lawn or in the back yard. You could buy them quite cheaply in any pet-shop and they were probably the least troublesome of all childhood pets, and quite harmless.

Tortoises used to be brought into England by the thousand, packed in crates, and they came mostly from North Africa. But not many years ago a law was passed that made it illegal to bring any tortoises into the country. This was not done to protect us. The little tortoise was not a danger to anybody. It was done purely out of kindness to the tortoise itself. You see, the traders who brought them in used to cram hundreds of them tightly into the packing-crates without food or water and in such horrible conditions that a great many of them always died on the sea-journey over. So rather than allow this cruelty to go on, the Government stopped the whole business.

The things you are going to read about in this story all happened in the days when anyone could go out and buy a nice little tortoise from a pet-shop.

ESIO TROT

Mr Hoppy lived in a small flat high up in a tall concrete building. He lived alone. He had always been a lonely man and now that he was retired from work he was more lonely than ever.

There were two loves in Mr Hoppy's life. One was the flowers he grew on his balcony. They grew in pots and tubs and baskets, and in summer the little balcony became a riot of colour.

Mr Hoppy's second love was a secret he kept entirely to himself.

The balcony immediately below Mr Hoppy's jutted out a good bit further from the building than his own, so Mr Hoppy always had a fine view of what was going on down there. This balcony belonged to an attractive middle-aged lady called Mrs Silver. Mrs Silver was a widow who also lived alone. And although she didn't know it, it was she who was the object of Mr Hoppy's secret love. He had loved her from his balcony for many years, but he was a very shy man and he had never been able to bring himself to give her even the smallest hint of his love.

Every morning, Mr Hoppy and Mrs Silver exchanged polite conversation, the one looking down from above, the other looking up, but that was as far as it ever went. The distance between their balconies might not have been more than a few yards, but to Mr Hoppy it seemed like a million miles. He longed to invite Mrs Silver up for a cup of tea and a biscuit, but every time he was about to form the words on his lips, his courage failed him. As I said, he was a very very shy man.

Oh, if only, he kept telling himself, if only he could do something tremendous like saving her life or rescuing her from a gang of armed thugs, if only he could perform some great feat that would make him a hero in her eyes. If only . . .

The trouble with Mrs Silver was that she gave all her love to somebody else, and that somebody was a small tortoise called Alfie. Every day, when Mr Hoppy looked over his balcony and saw Mrs Silver whispering endearments to Alfie and stroking his shell, he felt absurdly jealous. He wouldn't even have minded becoming a tortoise himself if it meant Mrs Silver stroking his shell each morning and whispering endearments to him.

Alfie had been with Mrs Silver for years and he lived on her balcony summer and winter. Planks had been placed around the sides of the balcony so that Alfie could walk about without toppling over the edge, and in one corner there was a little house into which Alfie would crawl every night to keep warm.

When the colder weather came along in November, Mrs Silver would fill Alfie's house with dry hay, and the tortoise would crawl in there and bury himself deep under the hay and go to sleep for months on end

without food or water. This is called hibernating.

In early spring, when Alfie felt the warmer weather through his shell, he would wake up and crawl very slowly out of his house on to the balcony. And Mrs Silver would clap her hands with joy and cry out, 'Welcome back, my darling one! Oh, how I have missed you!'

It was at times like these that Mr Hoppy wished more than ever that he could change places with Alfie and become a tortoise.

Now we come to a certain bright
morning in May when something
happened that changed and indeed
electrified Mr Hoppy's life. He was lean-
ing over his balcony-rail watching Mrs
Silver serving Alfie his breakfast.

'Here's the heart of the lettuce for you, my
lovely,' she was saying. 'And here's a slice of
fresh tomato and a piece of crispy celery.'

'Good morning, Mrs Silver,' Mr Hoppy said.
'Alfie's looking well this morning.'

'Isn't he gorgeous!' Mrs Silver said, looking up
and beaming at him.

'Absolutely gorgeous,' Mr Hoppy said, not meaning it. And now, as he looked down at Mrs Silver's smiling face gazing up into his own, he thought for the thousandth time how pretty she was, how sweet and gentle and full of kindness, and his heart ached with love.

'I do so wish he would *grow* a little faster,' Mrs
Silver was saying. 'Every spring, when he wakes up
from his winter sleep, I weigh him on the kitchen
scales. And do you know that in all the eleven years
I've had him he's not gained more than *three ounces*!
That's almost *nothing*!'

'What does he weigh now?' Mr Hoppy asked her.

'Just thirteen ounces,' Mrs Silver answered.
'About as much as a grapefruit.'

'Yes, well, tortoises are very slow growers,' Mr
Hoppy said solemnly. 'But they can live for a
hundred years.'

'I know that,' Mrs Silver said. 'But I do so wish
he would grow just a little bit bigger. He's such a
tiny wee fellow.'

'He seems just fine as he is,' Mr Hoppy said.

'No, he's *not* just fine!' Mrs Silver cried. 'Try to

think how miserable it must make him feel to be so titchy! Everyone wants to grow up.'

'You really *would* love him to grow bigger, wouldn't you?' Mr Hoppy said, and even as he said it his mind suddenly went *click* and an amazing idea came rushing into his head.

'Of course I would!' Mrs Silver cried. 'I'd give *anything* to make it happen! Why, I've seen pictures of giant tortoises that are so huge people can ride on their backs! If Alfie were to see those he'd turn green with envy!'

Mr Hoppy's mind was spinning like a fly-wheel. Here, surely, was his big chance! Grab it, he told himself. Grab it quick!

'Mrs Silver,' he said. 'I do actually happen to know how to make tortoises grow faster, if that's really what you want.'

'You do?' she cried. 'Oh, please tell me! Am I feeding him the wrong things?'

'I worked in North Africa once,' Mr Hoppy said. 'That's where all these tortoises in England come from, and a bedouin tribesman told me the secret.'

'Tell me!' cried Mrs Silver. 'I beg you to tell me, Mr Hoppy! I'll be your slave for life.'

When he heard the words *your slave for life*, a little shiver of excitement swept through Mr Hoppy. 'Wait there,' he said. 'I'll have to go in and write something down for you.'

In a couple of minutes Mr Hoppy was back on the balcony with a sheet of paper in his hand. 'I'm going to lower it to you on a bit of string,' he said, 'or it might blow away. Here it comes.'

Mrs Silver caught the paper and held it up in front of her. This is what she read:

ESIO TROT, ESIO TROT,
TEG REGGIB REGGIB!
EMOC NO, ESIO TROT,
WORG PU, FFUP PU, TOOHS PU!
GNIRPS PU, WOLB PU, LLEWS PU!
EGROG! ELZZUG! FFUTS! PLUG!
TUP NO TAF, ESIO TROT, TUP NO TAF!
TEG NO, TEG NO! ELBBOG DOOF!

'What *does* it mean?' she asked. 'Is it another language?'

'It's tortoise language,' Mr Hoppy said.

17

'Tortoises are very backward creatures. Therefore they can only understand words that are written backwards. That's obvious, isn't it?'

'I suppose so,' Mrs Silver said, bewildered.

'Esio trot is simply tortoise spelled backwards,' Mr Hoppy said. 'Look at it.'

'So it is,' Mrs Silver said.

'The other words are spelled backwards, too,' Mr Hoppy said. 'If you turn them round into human language, they simply say:

TORTOISE, TORTOISE,
GET BIGGER BIGGER!
COME ON, TORTOISE,
GROW UP, PUFF UP, SHOOT UP!
SPRING UP, BLOW UP, SWELL UP!
GORGE! GUZZLE! STUFF! GULP!
PUT ON FAT, TORTOISE, PUT ON FAT!
GET ON, GET ON! GOBBLE FOOD!'

Mrs Silver examined the magic words on the paper more closely. 'I guess you're right,' she said. 'How clever. But there's an awful lot of poos in it. Are they something special?'

'Poo is a very strong word in any language,' Mr Hoppy said, 'especially with tortoises. Now what you have to do, Mrs Silver, is hold Alfie up to your face and whisper these words to him three times a day, morning, noon and night. Let me hear you practise them.'

Very slowly and stumbling a little over the strange words, Mrs Silver read the whole message out loud in tortoise language.

'Not bad,' Mr Hoppy said. 'But try to get a little more expression into it when you say it to Alfie. If you do it properly I'll bet you anything you like that in a few months' time he'll be twice as big as he is now.'

'I'll try it,' Mrs Silver said. 'I'll try anything. Of course I will. But I can't believe it'll work.'

'You wait and see,' Mr Hoppy said, smiling at her.

Back in his flat, Mr Hoppy was simply quivering all over with excitement. *Your slave for life*, he kept repeating to himself. What bliss!

But there was a lot of work to be done before that happened.

The only furniture in Mr Hoppy's small living-room was a table and two chairs. These he moved into his bedroom. Then he went out and bought a sheet of thick canvas and spread it over the entire living-room floor to protect his carpet.

Next, he got out the telephone-book and wrote down the address of every pet-shop in the city. There were fourteen of them altogether.

It took him two days to visit each pet-shop and choose his tortoises. He wanted a great many, at least one hundred, perhaps more. And he had to choose them very carefully.

To you and me there is not much difference between one tortoise and another. They differ only in their size and in the colour of their shells. Alfie had a darkish shell, so Mr Hoppy chose only the darker-shelled tortoises for his great collection.

Size, of course, was everything. Mr Hoppy chose all sorts of different sizes, some weighing only slightly more than Alfie's thirteen ounces, others a great deal more, but he didn't want any that weighed less.

'Feed them cabbage leaves,' the pet-shop owners told him. 'That's all they'll need. And a bowl of water.'

When he had finished, Mr Hoppy, in his
enthusiasm, had bought no less than one hundred
and forty tortoises and he carried them home in
baskets, ten or fifteen at a time. He had to make a
lot of trips and he was quite exhausted at the end
of it all, but it was worth it. Boy, was it worth it!
And what an amazing sight his living-room was
when they were all in there together! The floor
was swarming with tortoises of different sizes,

some walking slowly about and exploring, some munching cabbage leaves, others drinking water from a big shallow dish. They made just the faintest rustling sound as they moved over the canvas sheet, but that was all. Mr Hoppy had to pick his way carefully on his toes between this moving sea of brown shells whenever he walked across the room. But enough of that. He must get on with the job.

Before he retired Mr Hoppy had been a mechanic in a bus-garage. And now he went back to his old place of work and asked his mates if he might use his old bench for an hour or two.

What he had to do now was to make something that would reach down from his own balcony to Mrs Silver's balcony and pick up a tortoise. This was not difficult for a mechanic like Mr Hoppy.

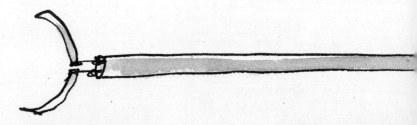

First he made two metal claws or fingers, and
these he attached to the end of a long metal tube.
He ran two stiff wires down inside the tube and
connected them to the metal claws in such a way
that when you pulled the wires, the claws closed,
and when you pushed them, the claws opened. The
wires were joined to a handle at the other end of
the tube. It was all very simple.

Mr Hoppy was ready to begin.

Mrs Silver had a part-time job. She worked from noon until five o'clock every weekday afternoon in a shop that sold newspapers and sweets. That made things a lot easier for Mr Hoppy.

So on that first exciting afternoon, after he had made sure that Mrs Silver had gone to work, Mr Hoppy went out on to his balcony armed with his long metal pole. He called this his tortoise-catcher. He leaned over the balcony railings and lowered the pole down on to Mrs Silver's balcony below. Alfie was basking in the pale sunlight over to one side.

'Hello, Alfie,' Mr Hoppy said. 'You are about to go for a little ride.'

He wiggled the tortoise-catcher till it was right above Alfie. He pushed the hand-lever so that the claws opened wide. Then he lowered the two claws neatly over Alfie's shell and pulled the lever. The claws closed tightly over the shell like two fingers of a hand. He hauled Alfie up on to his own balcony. It was easy.

Mr Hoppy weighed Alfie on his own kitchen scales just to make sure that Mrs Silver's figure of thirteen ounces was correct. It was.

Now, holding Alfie in one hand, he picked his way carefully through his huge collection of tortoises to find one that first of all had the same colour shell as Alfie's and secondly weighed *exactly two ounces more*.

Two ounces is not much. It is less than a smallish hen's egg weighs. But, you see, the important thing in Mr Hoppy's plan was to make sure that the new tortoise was bigger than Alfie but only a *tiny bit* bigger. The difference had to be so small that Mrs Silver wouldn't notice it.

From his vast collection, it was not difficult for Mr Hoppy to find just the tortoise he wanted. He wanted one that weighed fifteen ounces exactly on his kitchen scales, no more and no less. When he had got it, he put it on the kitchen table beside Alfie, and even he could hardly tell that one was bigger than the other. But it *was* bigger. It was bigger by two ounces. This was Tortoise Number 2.

Mr Hoppy took Tortoise Number 2 out on to the balcony and gripped it in the claws of his tortoise-catcher. Then he lowered it on to Mrs Silver's balcony, right beside a nice fresh lettuce.

Tortoise Number 2 had never eaten tender juicy lettuce leaves before. It had only had thick old cabbage leaves. It loved the lettuce and started chomping away at it with great gusto.

There followed a rather nervous two hours' wait for Mrs Silver to return from work.

Would she see any difference between the new tortoise and Alfie? It was going to be a tense moment.

Out on to her balcony swept Mrs Silver.

'Alfie, my darling!' she cried out. 'Mummy's back! Have you missed me?'

Mr Hoppy, peering over his railing, but well hidden between two huge potted plants, held his breath.

The new tortoise was still chomping away at the lettuce.

'My my, Alfie, you do seem hungry today,' Mrs Silver was saying. 'It must be Mr Hoppy's magic words I've been whispering to you.'

Mr Hoppy watched as Mrs Silver picked the tortoise up and stroked his shell. Then she fished Mr Hoppy's piece of paper out of her pocket, and holding the tortoise very close to her face, she whispered, reading from the paper:

'ESIO TROT, ESIO TROT,
TEG REGGIB REGGIB!
EMOC NO, ESIO TROT,
WORG PU, FFUP PU, TOOHS PU!
GNIRPS PU, WOLB PU, LLEWS PU!
EGROG! ELZZUG! FFUTS! PLUG!
TUP NO TAF, ESIO TROT, TUP NO TAF!
TEG NO, TEG NO! ELBBOG DOOF!'

Mr Hoppy
popped his head
out of the foliage
and called out,
'Good evening,
Mrs Silver. How
is Alfie tonight?'

'Oh, he's lovely,' Mrs Silver said, looking up and beaming. 'And he's developing *such* an appetite! I've never seen him eat like this before! It must be the magic words.'

'You never know,' Mr Hoppy said darkly. 'You never know.'

Mr Hoppy waited seven whole days before he made his next move.

On the afternoon of the seventh day, when Mrs Silver was at work, he lifted Tortoise Number 2 from the balcony below and brought it into his living-room. Number 2 had weighed exactly *fifteen* ounces. He must now find one that weighed exactly *seventeen* ounces, two ounces more.

From his enormous collection, he easily found a seventeen-ounce tortoise and once again he made sure the shells matched in colour. Then he lowered Tortoise Number 3 on to Mrs Silver's balcony.

As you will have guessed by now, Mr Hoppy's secret was a very simple one. If a creature grows slowly enough – I mean very very slowly indeed – then you'll never notice that it has grown at all, especially if you see it every day.

It's the same with children. They are actually growing taller every week, but their mothers never notice it until they grow out of their clothes.

Slowly does it, Mr Hoppy told himself. Don't hurry it.

So this is how things went over the next eight weeks.

In the beginning

ALFIE   weight 13 ounces

End of first week

TORTOISE NO. 2   weight 15 ounces

End of second week

TORTOISE NO. 3   weight 17 ounces

End of third week

TORTOISE NO. 4   weight 19 ounces

End of fourth week

TORTOISE NO. 5   weight 21 ounces

End of fifth week

TORTOISE NO. 6   weight 23 ounces

End of sixth week

TORTOISE NO. 7   weight 25 ounces

End of seventh week

TORTOISE NO. 8   weight 27 ounces

Alfie's weight was thirteen ounces. Tortoise Number 8 was twenty-seven ounces. Very slowly, over seven weeks, Mrs Silver's pet had more than doubled in size and the good lady hadn't noticed a thing.

Even to Mr Hoppy, peering down over his railing, Tortoise Number 8 looked pretty big. It was amazing that Mrs Silver had hardly noticed anything at all during the great operation. Only once had she looked up and said, 'You know, Mr Hoppy, I do believe he's getting a bit bigger. What do you think?'

'I can't see a lot of difference myself,' Mr Hoppy had answered casually.

But now perhaps it was time to call a halt, and that evening Mr Hoppy was just about to go out and suggest to Mrs Silver that she ought to weigh Alfie when a startled cry from the balcony below brought him outside fast.

'Look!' Mrs Silver was shouting. 'Alfie's too big to get through the door of his little house! He must have grown enormously!'

'Weigh him,' Mr Hoppy ordered. 'Take him in and weigh him quick.'

Mrs Silver did just that, and in half a minute she
was back holding the tortoise in both hands and
waving it above her head and shouting, 'Guess
what, Mr Hoppy! Guess what! He weighs twenty-
seven ounces! He's twice as big as he was before!
Oh, you darling!' she cried, stroking the tortoise.
'Oh, you great big wonderful boy! Just look what
clever Mr Hoppy has done for you!'

Mr Hoppy suddenly felt very brave. 'Mrs Silver,' he said. 'Do you think I could pop down to your balcony and hold Alfie myself?'

'Why, of course you can!' Mrs Silver cried. 'Come down at once.'

Mr Hoppy rushed down the stairs and Mrs Silver opened the door to him. Together they went out on to the balcony. 'Just look at him!' Mrs Silver said proudly. 'Isn't he grand!'

'He's a big good-sized tortoise now,' Mr Hoppy said.

'And *you* did it!' Mrs Silver cried. 'You're a miracle-man, you are indeed!'

'But what *am* I going to do about his house?' Mrs Silver said. 'He must have a house to go into at night, but now he can't get through the door.'

They were standing on the balcony looking at the tortoise, who was trying to push his way into his house. But he was too big.

'I shall have to enlarge the door,' Mrs Silver said.

'Don't do that,' Mr Hoppy said. 'You mustn't go chopping up such a pretty little house. After all, he only needs to be just a tiny bit smaller and he could get in easily.'

'How can he possibly get smaller?' Mrs Silver asked.

'That's simple,' Mr Hoppy said. 'Change the

magic words. Instead of telling him to get bigger
and bigger, tell him to get a bit smaller. But in
tortoise language of course.'

'Will that work?'

'Of course it'll work.'

'Tell me exactly what I have to say, Mr Hoppy.'

Mr Hoppy got out a piece of paper and a pencil
and wrote:

ESIO TROT, ESIO TROT,
TEG A TIB RELLAMS, A TIB RELLAMS.

'That'll do it, Mrs Silver,' he said, handing her the paper.

'I don't mind trying it,' Mrs Silver said. 'But look here, I wouldn't want him to get titchy small all over again, Mr Hoppy.'

'He won't, dear lady, he won't,' Mr Hoppy said. 'Say it only tonight and tomorrow morning and then see what happens. We might be lucky.'

'If it works,' Mrs Silver said, touching him softly on the arm, 'then you are the cleverest man alive.'

The next afternoon, as soon as Mrs Silver had gone to work, Mr Hoppy lifted the tortoise up from her balcony and carried it inside. All he had to do now was to find one that was a shade smaller, so that it would just go through the door of the little house.

He chose one and lowered it down with his tortoise-catcher. Then, still gripping the tortoise, he tested it to see if it would go through the door. It wouldn't.

He chose another. Again he tested it. This one went through nicely. Good. He placed the tortoise in the middle of the balcony beside a nice piece of lettuce and went inside to await Mrs Silver's home-coming.

That evening, Mr Hoppy was watering his plants on the balcony when suddenly he heard Mrs Silver's shouts from below, shrill with excitement.

'Mr Hoppy! Mr Hoppy! Where are you?' she was shouting. 'Just look at this!'

Mr Hoppy popped his head over the railing and said, 'What's up?'

'Oh, Mr Hoppy, it's worked!' she was crying. 'Your magic words have worked again on Alfie! He can now get through the door of his little house! It's a miracle!'

'Can I come down and look?' Mr Hoppy shouted back.

'Come down at once, my dear man!' Mrs Silver answered. 'Come down and see the wonders you have worked upon my darling Alfie!'

Mr
Hoppy
turned and
ran from the
balcony into the
living-room, jumping
on tip-toe like a ballet-
dancer between the sea of
tortoises that covered the floor. He
flung open his front door and flew down
the stairs two at a time with the love-songs of
a thousand cupids ringing in his ears. *This is it!*
he whispered to himself under his breath. *The greatest
moment of my life is coming up now! I mustn't bish it. I
mustn't bosh it! I must keep very calm!* When he was
three-quarters way down the stairs he caught sight
of Mrs Silver already standing at the open door
waiting to welcome him with a huge smile on her
face. She flung her arms around him and cried out,
'You really are the most wonderful man I've ever
met! You can do anything! Come in at once and let
me make you a cup of tea. That's the very least you
deserve!'

Seated in a comfortable armchair in Mrs Silver's
parlour, sipping his tea, Mr Hoppy was all of a twit-
ter. He looked at the lovely lady sitting opposite him
and smiled at her. She smiled right back at him.

That smile of hers, so warm and friendly, suddenly gave him the courage he needed, and he said, 'Mrs Silver, please will you marry me?'

'Why, Mr Hoppy!' she cried. 'I didn't think you'd ever get round to asking me! Of course I'll marry you!'

Mr Hoppy got rid of his teacup and the two of them stood up and embraced warmly in the middle of the room.

'It's all due to Alfie,' Mrs Silver said, slightly breathless.

'Good old Alfie,' Mr Hoppy said. 'We'll keep him for ever.'

The next afternoon, Mr Hoppy took all his other tortoises back to the pet-shops and said they could have them for nothing. Then he cleaned up his living-room, leaving not a leaf of cabbage nor a trace of tortoise.

A few weeks later, Mrs Silver became Mrs Hoppy and the two of them lived very happily ever after.

P.S. I expect you are wondering what happened to little Alfie, the first of them all. Well, he was bought a week later from one of the pet-shops by a small girl called Roberta Squibb, and she settled down in Roberta's garden. Every day she fed him lettuce and tomato slices and crispy celery, and in the winters he hibernated in a box of dried leaves in the tool-shed.

That was a long time ago. Roberta has grown up and is now married and has two children of her own. She lives in another house, but Alfie is still with her, still the much-loved family pet, and Roberta reckons that by now he must be about thirty years old. It has taken him all that time to grow to twice the size he was when Mrs Silver had him. But he made it in the end.

A Day in the Life of
ROALD DAHL

Roald Dahl had a very strict daily routine. He would eat breakfast in bed and open his post. At 10.30 a.m. he would walk through the garden to his writing hut and work until 12 p.m. when he went back to the house for lunch – typically, a gin and tonic followed by Norwegian prawns with mayonnaise and lettuce. At the end of every meal, Roald and his family had a chocolate bar chosen from a red plastic box.

After a snooze, he would take a flask of tea back to the writing hut and work from 4 p.m. till 6 p.m. He would be back at the house at exactly six o'clock, ready for his dinner.

He always wrote in pencil and only ever used a very particular kind of yellow pencil with a rubber on the end. Before he started writing, Roald made sure he had six sharpened pencils in a jar by his side. They lasted for two hours before needing to be resharpened.

Roald was *very* particular about the kind of paper he used as well. He wrote all of his books on American yellow legal pads, which were sent to him from New York. He wrote and rewrote until he was sure that every word was just right. A lot of yellow paper was thrown away. Once a month, when his large wastepaper basket was full to overflowing, he made a bonfire just outside his writing hut (where one of the white walls was soon streaked with black soot).

Once Roald had finished writing a book, he gave the pile of yellow scribbled paper to Wendy, his secretary, and she turned it into a neat printed manuscript to send to his publisher.

GOBBLEFUNK

Roald Dahl loved playing around with words and inventing new ones. In *The BFG* he gave this strange language an even stranger name – Gobblefunk!

BAGGLEPIPES

Bagpipes: famous Scottish wind instrument.

BOGGLEBOX

A school for young children (generally boys).

CRABCRUNCHER

Crabcrunchers live high up on cliffs by the sea. They're very rare.

FROTHBUNGLING

Means stupid.

GLORIUMPTIOUS

Gloriously wonderful.

HUMAN BEAN

This is the name the giants in *The BFG* give to human beings.

JUMPSQUIFFLING

Something absolutely huge.

LIXIVATE

Very gruesome! You are squashed and turned to liquid at the same time.

MUGGLED

To be muggled means to be a bit confused.

QUOGWINKLE

A quogwinkle is an alien from outer space.

SNITCHING

Stealing and thieving.

SNOZZCUMBER

The BFG is forced to eat this disgusting vegetable as it is the only thing that grows in Giant Country. It's knobbly, with black and white stripes, and tastes horrible!

TROGGLEHUMPER

The worst kind of dream: a nightmare.

QUENTINBLAKE

'The finest illustrator of children's books in the world today!' – Roald Dahl

Roald Dahl and Quentin Blake make a perfect partnership of words and illustrations, but when Roald started writing he had many different illustrators. Quentin started working with him in 1976 (the first book he illustrated was *The Enormous Crocodile*, published in 1978) and from then on they worked together until Roald's death. Quentin ended up illustrating all of Roald Dahl's books, with the exception of *The Minpins*.

To begin with, Quentin was a bit nervous about working with such a very famous author, but by the time they collaborated on *The BFG* they had become firm friends. Quentin never knew anything about a new story until the manuscript arrived. 'You'll have some fun with this,' Roald would say – or, 'You'll have some trouble with this.' Quentin would make lots of rough drawings to take along to Gipsy House, where he would show them to Roald and see what he thought. Roald Dahl liked his books to be packed with illustrations – Quentin ended up drawing twice as many pictures for *The BFG* as he had originally been asked for.

Quentin Blake's favourite Roald Dahl book is *The BFG*. When he wasn't quite sure what the BFG's footwear would look like, Roald actually sent one of his old sandals through the post to Quentin – and that's what he drew!

Quentin Blake was born on 16 December 1932. His first drawing was published when he was sixteen, and he has written and illustrated many of his own books, as well as Roald Dahl's. Besides being an illustrator he taught for over twenty years at the Royal College of Art and in 1999 he became the first ever Children's Laureate! Six years later he was awarded a CBE for services to children's literature and in 2013 he was knighted in the New Year's Honours – which means his full title is Sir Quentin Blake, although we can all still go on calling him Quentin as usual.

Find out more at quentinblake.com

Wish you were here...

EASTER

Roald Dahl's father died when Roald was only three so his mother brought up him and his sisters on her own. Every Easter she rented a house in Tenby, Wales, and took all the children there for a holiday. The house, called The Cabin, was right next to the sea. When the tide was in, the waves broke right up against one wall of the house. Roald and his sisters used to collect winkles and eat them on slices of bread and butter.

Best of all were the summer holidays. From the time he was four years old to when he was seventeen, Roald and his family went to Norway every summer. There were no commercial aeroplanes in those days, so the journey was a splendid expedition. It took four days to get there, and four days to get back again! The sea crossing from Newcastle to Oslo lasted two days and a night – and Roald was generally seasick.

Finally, they would reach what Roald Dahl called 'the magic island', the island of Tjøme in a Norwegian fjord. The family would swim and sunbathe, mess about in rock pools, and go fishing. When Roald was seven, his mother acquired a motor boat and they could explore other islands.

'We would cling to the sides of our funny little white motor boat, driving through mountainous white-capped waves and getting drenched to the skin, while my mother calmly handled the tiller. There were times, I promise you, when the waves were so high that as we slid down into a trough the whole world disappeared from sight . . . It requires great skill to handle a small boat in seas like these . . . But my mother knew exactly how to do it, and we were never afraid.'

Weird and wonderful facts about

ROALD DAHL

He was very tall – six feet five and three-quarter inches, or nearly two metres. His nickname in the RAF was Lofty, while Walt Disney called him Stalky (because he was like a beanstalk!).

His nickname at home was the Apple, because he was the apple of his mother's eye (which means her favourite!).

He pretended to have appendicitis when he was nine because he was so homesick in his first two weeks at boarding school. He fooled the matron and the school doctor and was sent home. But he couldn't fool his own doctor, who made him promise never to do it again.

He was a terrible speller, but he liked playing Scrabble.

He didn't like cats – but he did like dogs, birds and goats.

Roald Dahl wrote the screenplay for the James Bond film *You Only Live Twice*.

He once had a tame magpie.

He was a keen photographer at school and, when he was eighteen, won two prizes: one from the Royal Photographic Society in London and another from the Photographic Society of Holland.

THERE'S MORE TO ROALD DAHL
THAN GREAT STORIES . . .

Did you know that 10% of author royalties* from this book go to help the work of the Roald Dahl charities?

Roald Dahl's Marvellous Children's Charity exists to make life better for seriously ill children because it believes that every child has the right to a marvellous life. This marvellous charity helps thousands of children each year living with serious conditions of the blood and the brain – causes important to Roald Dahl in his lifetime – whether by providing nurses, equipment or toys for today's children in the UK, or helping tomorrow's children everywhere through pioneering research.

Can you do something marvellous to help others? Find out how at **www.roalddahlcharity.org**

The Roald Dahl Museum and Story Centre, based in Great Missenden just outside London, is in the Buckinghamshire village where Roald Dahl lived and wrote. At the heart of the Museum, created to inspire a love of reading and writing, is his unique archive of letters and manuscripts. As well as two fun-packed biographical galleries, the Museum boasts an interactive Story Centre and is now the home of his famous writing hut. It is a place for the family and teachers and their pupils to explore the exciting world of creativity and literacy.

Find out more at **www.roalddahlmuseum.org**

ROALD DAHL'S

WRITING TIPS

'A story idea is liable to come flitting into the mind at any moment of the day, and if I don't make a note of it at once, right then and there, it will be gone forever. So I must find a pencil, a pen, a crayon, a lipstick, anything that will write, and scribble a few words that will later on remind me of the idea. Then, as soon as I get the chance, I go straight to my hut and write the idea down in an old red-coloured school exercise book.'

Can you guess which book came from this idea?

What about a chocolate factory
That makes fantastic and marvellous
Things — with a crazy man running it?

Charlie and the Chocolate Factory

The reason I collect good ideas is because plots themselves are very difficult indeed to come by. Every month they get scarcer and scarcer. Any good story must start with a strong plot that gathers momentum all the way to the end. My main preoccupation when I am writing a story is a constant unholy terror of boring the reader. Consequently, as I write my stories I always try to create situations that will cause my reader to:

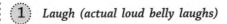

1. *Laugh (actual loud belly laughs)*

2. *Squirm*

3. *Become enthralled*

4. *Become TENSE and EXCITED and say, "Read on! Please read on! Don't stop!"*

All good books have to have a mixture of extremely nasty people – which are always fun – and some nice people. In every book or story there has to be somebody you can loathe. The fouler and more filthy a person is, the more fun it is to watch him getting scrunched.

ROALD DAHL'S

When Roald was sixteen, he decided to go off on his own to holiday in France. He crossed the Channel from Dover to Calais with £24 in his pocket (a lot of money in 1933). Roald wanted to see the Mediterranean Sea, so he took the train first to Paris, then on to Marseilles where he got on a bus that went all the way along the coastal road towards Monte Carlo. He finished up at a place called St Jean Cap Ferrat and stayed there for ten days, wandering around by himself and doing whatever he wanted. It was his first taste of absolute freedom – and what it was like to be a grown-up.

He travelled back home the same way, but by the time he reached Dover he had absolutely no money left. Luckily a fellow passenger gave him ten shillings (50p in today's money!) for his fare home. Roald never forgot this kindness and generosity.

When Roald was seventeen he signed up to go to Newfoundland, Canada, with 'The Public Schools' Exploring Society'. Together with thirty other boys, he spent three weeks trudging over a desolate landscape with an enormous rucksack. It weighed so much that he needed someone to help him hoist it on to his back every morning. The boys lived on pemmican (strips of pressed meat, fat, and berries) and lentils, and they experimented with eating boiled lichen and reindeer moss because they were so hungry. It was a genuine adventure and left Roald fit and ready for anything!

ROALD DAHL'S
SCHOOL REPORTS

In 1929, when he was thirteen, Roald Dahl was sent to boarding school. You would expect him to get wonderful marks in English – but his school reports were *not* good!

His end-of-term reports from this school are of some interest. Here are just four of them, copied word for word from the original documents:

SUMMER TERM, 1930 (aged 14).
English Composition.
'I have never met a boy who so persistently writes the exact opposite of what he means. He seems incapable of marshalling his thoughts on paper.'

EASTER TERM, 1931 (aged 15). ***English Composition.***
'A persistent muddler. Vocabulary negligible, sentences malconstructed. He reminds me of a camel.'

SUMMER TERM, 1932 (aged 16). ***English Composition.***
'This boy is an indolent and illiterate member of the class.'

AUTUMN TERM, 1932 (aged 17). ***English Composition.***
'Consistently idle. Ideas limited.'

'Little wonder that it never entered my head to become a writer in those days.'

Find out more about Roald Dahl at school in *Boy*.

ROALD DAHL SAYS

'I think probably kindness is my number one attribute in a human being. I'll put it before any of the things like courage or bravery or generosity or anything else. If you're kind, that's it.'

'I am totally convinced that most grown-ups have completely forgotten what it is like to be a child between the ages of five and ten . . . I can remember exactly what it was like. I am certain I can.'

'When I first thought about writing the book *Charlie and the Chocolate Factory*, I never originally meant to have children in it at all!'

'If I had my way, I would remove January from the calendar altogether and have an extra July instead.'

'You can write about anything for children as long as you've got humour.'

Take a tour of Roald Dahl's
scrumdiddlyumptious
official website with your
favourite characters at

roalddahl.com